What I'll Remember When I Am a Grownup

By Gina Willner-Pardo
Illustrated by Walter Lyon Krudop

CLARION BOOKS
New York

Clarion Books
a Houghton Mifflin Company imprint
215 Park Avenue South, New York, NY 10003
Text copyright © 1994 by Gina Willner-Pardo
Illustrations copyright © 1994 by Walter Lyon Krudop

Printed in the U.S.A.

Library of Congress Cataloging-in-Publication Data

Willner-Pardo, Gina.
What I'll remember when I am a grownup / by Gina Willner-Pardo;
illustrated by Walter Lyon Krudop.
p. cm.
Summary: During a weekend stay with his father and stepmother, a
young boy comes to terms with living with two separate but loving families.
ISBN 0-395-63310-9
1. Divorce—Fiction. I. Krudop, Walter, 1966- ill. II. Title.
PZ7.W68368Wh 1994
[E]—dc20 92-42148
CIP
AC

HOR 10 9 8 7 6 5 4 3 2 1

For Winnie and Gonzalo,
and, as always,
for Brian, Evan, and Cara.
— G. W.–P.

For my mother.
— W. L. K.

I.

I knew it wasn't going to be just any old weekend. I was going to Dad and Marilyn's, just like always. But Dad called me on Thursday. "Marilyn and I have something important to tell you this weekend, Dan," he said.

"What?" I asked.

"We want to tell you in person," Dad said.

Uh oh, I thought. Nobody ever wants to tell you anything good in person.

Dad asked me some stuff about school. I barely answered. Worrying was making it hard to concentrate.

On Friday, I was still worrying so much that I almost didn't see when Kevin Finelli shot a rubber band at creepy old Mrs. Silvera and knocked her wig off.

Everyone hated math when Mrs. Estes was sick. Even kids who liked math hated it without Mrs. Estes. Mrs. Silvera was always the math substitute, which was ridiculous, since she never did any math. She was too busy sending kids to the principal or folding her arms and looking at the floor and saying, "I'm waiting." Mrs. Silvera hated kids. She even said so. Actually, what she said was, "And I thought my own kids were monsters!" She said it quietly, but we all knew she wanted us to hear.

Kevin didn't knock her wig all the way off. Just halfway down her forehead. "I didn't even know you were wearing a wig!" he yelled as Mrs. Silvera yanked him into the hall. Which made her even madder.

On the way home from school, Kevin couldn't stop laughing.

"Wasn't it great, Dan?" he kept asking. "Wasn't it the funniest thing you ever saw?"

"It was pretty funny," I kept saying. It was. I knew I should feel sorry for Mrs. Silvera. But I didn't.

Kevin picked up a rock and threw it as high into the air as he could.

"That was the funniest thing I ever saw," he said. "I'll never forget it as long as I live."

That's what started me thinking. About what I'd remember when I was a grownup. I was pretty sure I wouldn't remember Mrs. Silvera losing her wig. If there was only enough room in my brain to remember a few things, I didn't want Mrs. Silvera in there taking up space.

"You know what I'll never forget?" I said to Kevin. "When the guys trapped Rodney Hurst out behind the bike racks and pinched him because he forgot to wear green on St. Patrick's Day."

"Oh, yeah," said Kevin. "I remember that."

"What I will mainly remember is how he didn't fight back," I said. "Because you're supposed to know about St. Patrick's Day and pinching."

"Yeah," said Kevin. "Rodney looked like he thought he had it coming."

We looked in the bushes for more rocks to throw. It was nice to take a break from worrying.

"Pork chops and brownies with nuts in them," Kevin said.

"What?"

"I'll always remember my grandma's cooking," Kevin said. "She makes the best pork chops I ever tasted. And brownies with nuts." He disappeared under a bush. "My mom always forgets to buy nuts," I heard him say.

"My dad makes the best spaghetti sauce in the world," I said. "With carrots and celery and tomatoes. He even puts a leaf in it, to make it taste better."

"A leaf?"

"Yeah." I found a rock, perfect-sized for throwing. "I like to sit on the counter and watch him put all the spaghetti stuff in the pot."

The rock felt smooth and cool in my hand. Too nice to let go of. I put it in my pocket. "I'll always remember doing that."

Suddenly I thought of something. What if Dad and Marilyn were going to move away? What if that was what they wanted to tell me?

I tried to remember where Marilyn's mom lived. I thought maybe it was Florida. Would I have to go to Florida every summer, the way Mary Frances Kinney had to go to Arizona to see her dad?

Or maybe it would be even worse. Maybe they would be too busy in Florida, with DisneyWorld and the Everglades and everything. Maybe they would tell me not to come at all.

Then who would I make spaghetti with?

Spaghetti reminded me of Joey Strazza. It felt better to think about Joey than to wonder about Dad and Marilyn.

"I know something else I will never forget," I said.

"What?" Kevin asked.

"The first time I met Joey Strazza. I was sitting on the curb outside my house. It was when I was six. He was only four, but he could stand on his head and balance a basketball on his feet. I saw him. It was unbelievable." I was quiet for a second, remembering. "He told me that once he was eating spaghetti and sneezed and a noodle came out his nose."

I was sitting on the curb because Mom and Dad were fighting inside. I didn't tell Kevin that, though.

"Wow," Kevin said.

"That was two years ago, and I still think about it."
My hand closed around the rock in my pocket. "I will
never forget it."

We started walking again.

"It's funny, the stuff you remember," Kevin said. I
could tell he was remembering something he wasn't
going to tell me.

I thought about my blanket, which Dad said I was too old for. It was in the hall closet at Dad and Marilyn's house. Mom liked me to keep my old things at Dad and Marilyn's because their house had lots of closets and ours hardly had any.

When I was little, I used to twist my blanket into a point and stick it in my ear. It made a good sound, soft and scratchy at the same time. I was sure that even when I was old, I would remember what it felt like to fall asleep with my blanket in my ear.

We came to where Kevin went right and I went left.

"I've got to hurry," I said. "My mom's taking me to my dad's."

I'd gotten pretty used to saying that.

"Maybe Mrs. Estes will be back on Monday," Kevin said.

"Keep your fingers crossed," I yelled, running across the street.

I thought about Dad and Marilyn. And wondered. Would they take my blanket to Florida?

II.

I could tell Mom was home the second I walked in the door. I couldn't see or hear her. But I could smell coffee. Mom always made coffee when she got home from work.

I stood in the hall and took deep breaths. Everything smelled so good that I forgot about worrying.

Smelling coffee reminded me of when I used to lie in bed listening to Mom and Dad play poker. "Deal the hand, Jack," Mom would say. The cards slapped against each other when Dad mixed them up. I could hear the bubbly sound of coffee being poured into a cup and Dad laughing at Mom's jokes.

"What's up, Daniel?" Mom asked. She put an apple muffin on a plate and poured some milk and made it chocolate.

I didn't want to tell her I was worried. If she didn't know what Dad and Marilyn had to tell me, she might worry, too. I was already doing enough worrying for both of us.

"Remember when you and Dad used to play poker?" I asked instead.

Mom's eyes looked happy with a little bit of sad in them. "Oh, yes," she said. "I remember that."

"I bet you don't remember what you used to say."

Mom laughed. "Go to sleep, Daniel," she pretended to yell. "We can hear you thinking."

That's another thing I'll remember when I am a grownup, I thought.

"You couldn't really hear me thinking," I said.

If grownups could really hear kids thinking, they wouldn't wait to tell them things in person.

"Of course not," Mom said. She was looking at me like she wanted to ask me something.

So that she wouldn't, I asked, "What do you remember from when you were a kid?"

Mom smiled. "I loved school. I remember recess and fire drills and spelling bees. I remember the volcano I made for the fourth grade science fair. And shopping for school clothes the last week of summer vacation."

I loved summer vacation, except last year, when Mom and Dad and the lawyers were figuring out where I would live. Last summer I spent a lot of time doing nothing. I didn't feel like swimming or playing baseball or riding my bike to the drugstore for ice cream.

I spent a whole afternoon watching ants crawl in and out of a crack in the sidewalk. Actually, I wondered a lot about those ants. Did they know each other? Could they tell each other apart? Did ants have families? Did they live with them, or just with anybody?

Now that I thought about it, I was sure I would never forget watching those ants.

"I will always remember my ElectroRoad Racer and my bike and my walkie-talkie and my bear and my shell collection and my wooden dinosaur model," I said, swallowing my last bite of muffin.

"I always liked that dinosaur model," Mom said. She looked at her watch.

I had to ask. "So, what do they want to tell me?"

Then I blew bubbles into my milk, so she wouldn't think I was too interested.

"They want to tell you themselves, Daniel," Mom said. "I have to let them do that."

So she did know after all. Why wouldn't she tell me? Maybe it was so bad that she didn't want to be the one to break it to me.

And then I thought of something else. What if Dad and Marilyn weren't moving to Florida? What if they wanted to tell me they were getting a divorce?

I choked a little on my milk.

"Daniel." Mom was looking at me. "If I *could* have heard you thinking just now," she asked, "what would I have heard?"

I stood up and took my plate and glass to the sink. I remembered the soft, warm light at the end of the dark hall, the coffee smell, how they sounded, laughing.

"That I don't like being left out," I said.

Mom was quiet. After a minute, she said, "Dad and Marilyn want to tell you themselves because they don't want to leave you out." She came over to the sink and hugged me. "Can you see that?"

"Yeah," I said, even though I couldn't.

Still, it was nice being hugged.

I remembered the time I opened Mom's door without knocking and saw her crying. Dad and Marilyn got married the next weekend. I didn't want to go to the wedding, but Mom said I had to.

"O.K.," Mom said. "Get your stuff. It's time to go."

Upstairs, I threw an extra pair of socks into my day pack. I thought about Dad and Marilyn getting

divorced. Would Marilyn just leave? Would I ever see her again?

The first time I met Marilyn was when she and Dad took me to the zoo. I lied and said all I wanted to see were the snakes. I thought maybe Marilyn didn't like snakes.

As I zipped up my pack, I thought that I'd never forget those snakes, which I stared at so I wouldn't have to see Dad and Marilyn holding hands.

III.

Dad chopped the carrots. I stirred everything in the pot. Marilyn gave me a soda to drink.

"Making spaghetti is thirsty work," she said.

I kept sneaking looks at them. To see if I could tell anything.

I could tell they were sneaking looks at each other. It was like their eyes were asking, Is now a good time? My stomach knotted up.

I tried to think of a way of finding out about Marilyn and Florida. "Have you ever been to DisneyWorld?" I asked. I didn't want to ask where Marilyn's mom lived. I didn't want to be too obvious.

"No," she said. "I don't like rides. Too up-and-down for me."

I thought about this for a while. It didn't really tell me anything. But somehow it made me feel better.

I couldn't think of how to ask about a divorce.

"Remember the Boardwalk, Daniel?" Dad asked.

I smiled into my soda. The Boardwalk was one of Dad's favorite stories.

"You should have seen him," Dad said to Marilyn. "He was afraid of the Cyclone, and I said, 'Just try. Just give it a try.' And he did. And he loved it. He rode it five, maybe six times. We had to pull him off, kicking and screaming."

Dad wasn't a hugger. That's what Mom always said. I knew Dad told the Boardwalk story instead of hugging.

He looked into the pot.

"Hey, Daniel, how's that look to you?"

"Good," I said.

"I'd say that looks like the greatest pot of spaghetti sauce the world has ever seen!" Dad said.

Marilyn and I laughed. I thought, Mom and Dad didn't laugh at all when *they* were getting divorced.

Dad and Marilyn laughed all through dinner. They sure didn't act like people with bad news.

All the same, I just couldn't ask them what they wanted to tell me. I just couldn't.

I was too scared.

They ended up not telling me at dinner. They waited until I'd brushed my teeth and gotten under the covers. It was funny, both of them sitting on my bed at once. There almost wasn't room for me.

Dad did all the talking. He told me everything while Marilyn rubbed my back. How it wouldn't be until

November. How the doctor said it was a boy. How they
knew it would take a while to get used to the idea.

Dad flipped off the light.

"Big day, huh?" he asked. "I bet this is a day you'll
remember for a long time."

"I don't know," I said.

Just before I fell asleep, I remembered when I spent the night at Kevin's house. We had pizza for dinner and chocolate sundaes for dessert. When I asked if I had to eat a vegetable before my ice cream, Mrs. Finelli said I had green peppers on my pizza and that was enough.

We slept on the floor in sleeping bags. I woke up once. I started being homesick and I almost called for Mr. Finelli to take me home. Then I felt Kevin's dog Jasper next to me, all stretched out. I rolled over and put my arm around him. He smelled like the inside of a car on a rainy day.

I was sure I'd never forget that smell.

I fell asleep wishing I had Jasper to hold on to.

IV.

"I remember when my little brother and I used to play hookey from Sunday school," Marilyn said, punching her mitt.

We were having a picnic in the park down the street. Dad had fallen asleep on the grass.

I threw Marilyn the softball. "You? Hookey?"

"We hid out in a drainage ditch behind the church. We told jokes. We talked." Marilyn threw the ball back. "Memories are always better with brothers in them."

I don't know about always, I thought.

"Didn't you hate him sometimes?" I asked. I didn't mean for this to come out. I didn't even know I was wondering about it. It kind of scared me.

"Sometimes being mad at someone feels like hating," Marilyn said. "It isn't the same thing."

We threw the ball some more.

"Didn't you feel left out?" I asked. I dropped the ball and it rolled under some bushes. Hunting for it, I was glad she couldn't see my face.

"I guess so. Sometimes," Marilyn said. "But having a brother made me feel like part of something, too. I wasn't just somebody's kid. I was somebody's sister."

Hey, I thought.

But I wasn't ready to be cheered up yet. What if I had to share my room?

"But," I said. And it came out before I could stop it. "I won't be the only one anymore."

It was everything I could do to keep myself from crying.

"No," Marilyn said. She was quiet for a while. Then she said, "But you'll always be the only Daniel. You'll always be the one who rode the Cyclone and had to be pulled off, kicking and screaming.

"And someday, your little brother will beg us to take him to the Boardwalk so he can ride the Cyclone with you." Marilyn patted her stomach with her mitt. "And he'll remember it forever."

I thought about that. Was I going to be something my brother remembered when he was a grownup?

I decided not to ask about sharing a room. I didn't have to know right then. I had enough to worry about. Like whether he was going to follow me around all the time. Whether he would want to borrow all my things. Whether he would be the kind of kid who would talk my head off. Or the kind who would like to ride bikes to the drugstore for ice cream.

It wasn't worrying, actually. Worrying was what I'd been doing since Thursday. It was more like wondering.

It was a funny time to remember my nightmare. In it, Mrs. Silvera was chasing me through the halls. I knew I had done something to make her mad. I knew I had it coming. I woke up crying.

I was pretty sure I wouldn't always remember the nightmare. But I knew I'd never forget Marilyn sitting on the bed saying, "It's all right, Daniel, honey," over and over. Or when she got up and walked down the hall.

I heard her poking around in the closet, and I knew what she was looking for.

I kept crying, though, until I had twisted my blanket into a point and stuck it in my ear.

I thought about that until I heard Marilyn saying, "O.K., Dan, let's see your fastball."

I threw the fastest fastball I had in me. "I wish there was only good stuff to remember," I said. "But I know it's not like that."

"No," said Marilyn, "it's not."

"Everyone thinks you remember the big things," I said.

"But you don't," said Marilyn.

"I think I will remember little things," I said. "How things sound. How they smell."

"How they feel," said Marilyn.

She threw a high fastball, and I caught it. Even when I am a grownup, I think I will remember how that ball felt, hard and round, as I closed my glove around it.

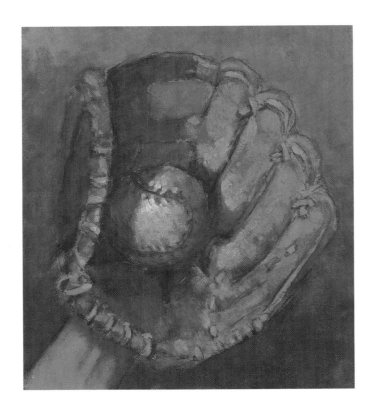

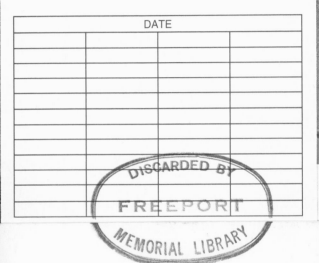